Jackie

WINS THEM ALL

Written by
Fabian E. Ferguson

Illustrations by
Alisa Aryutova

F. FERGUSON BOOKS

Today is the day of the big city race,

and the middle school is buzzing on Albany Place.

Excitement and chatter fill the school's hall.

All talks are of Jackie, because she wins them all.

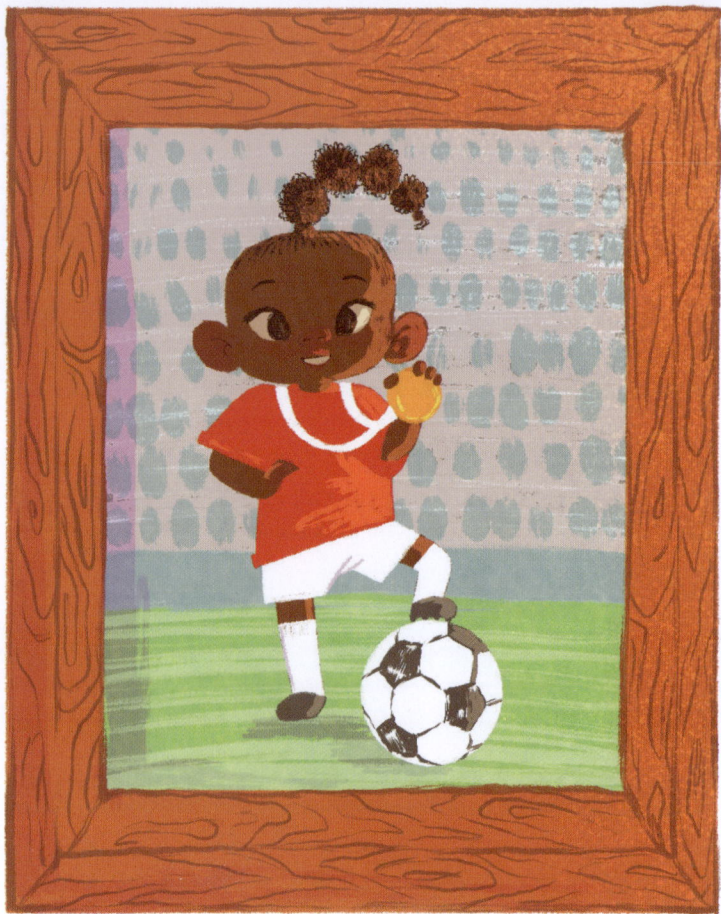

The amazingly talented Jackie J. Spade,

a star in the making in just the sixth grade!

A history of winning ever since she was three,
only losing baby teeth throughout the whole spree.

She's an all-star in tennis and swings a mean bat;
holds records in swimming and gym acrobats.

A science fair winner of not one, but two!

A spelling bee champion with HUL-LA-BA-LOO.

H-U-L-L-A-B-A-L-O-O

She has all kinds of trophies in her big trophy case;

a sight that's worth seeing when you visit her place.

She has gold ones, crystal ones, and sparkly ones too.

All color ribbons, from purple to blue.

Her success is well known; her name's common knowledge.

Especially after beating that one guy from college.

Not a loss in her history that one can recall.

Yup, Jackie's a legend because she wins them all!

Well, enough about Jackie, the race will soon start.

It is time for all runners to get set on their mark.

The crowd grows to silence, and the whispers get soft.

The runners are focused...

...AND THEY'RE OFF!

The racers huff and they puff, as they all try to beat her.
But they better act fast in this 200 meter.

Down the home stretch, sweat flies from her skin.

Crossing the finish line is Jackie...

...but she didn't win?!

Her mind flooding with questions—the hows, and the whys;

she drops down to her knees with tears in her eyes.

As she makes her way up from the sweat puddled dirt,

it was clear on her face just how bad this loss hurt.

She then dusts herself off and wipes tears from her face.

She walks right on over and says...

"Good Race!"

A hand, a hug, and some smiles were returned.

There were no hard feelings, just some hard lessons learned.

There are times you're on top; and times you will fall,

things won't always work out—you can't win them all.

Work hard, give your best, and do all you can do.

That's what matters most, and this Jackie knew!

One last walk past the crowd, and they all start to cheer.
Jackie smiles and responds, "I'll see you next year."

Walking tall and proud with all that's left in her;

sure, today Jackie lost, but she moves on like a winner.

For my daughter and nieces—
the most amazingly talented group of young girls.

Copyright © 2020 by Fabian E. Ferguson

Words and Design by Fabian E. Ferguson
Illustrations by Alisa Aryutova
Edited by Stephanie C. Lilavois

ISBN 978-0-578-75221-1
E-book 978-0-578-75223-5

Library of Congress Control Number: 2020944735

Printed in China

F. FERGUSON
BOOKS

110 Jabez Street #1124 Newark, NJ 07105
www.ffergusonbooks.com